Curly and the Log

Tony Mitton
Illustrated by Andy Parker

"Come up and play," said Curly.

"Up I come," said Ladybird.

"Up I come," said Grasshopper.

"Come on, Snail," they said.

"Help! Down I go!"
said Snail.

"Come down and play," said Snail.

"Down we come," they said.